Dead Silence

Aurelio Rico Lopez III

Cover artist: Nescel Giabia

For Kahil Lily, my everything.

Table of Contents

Dead Silence

Cole awoke smothered in darkness. For a panic-stricken moment, he thought he was back in San Vicente. He whimpered and kicked off his blanket.

Pulse racing, his eyes adjusted to the gloom. Gradually, the surrounding shapes began to look familiar – the wooden dresser against the wall, the chair at the foot of the bed, even the ugly bedside lamp to his left.

He blinked his eyes and groaned as he sat up. Damn. He was only twenty-eight, but it felt like he was pushing fifty.

Slowly, he swung his legs off the side of the bed and sat up. The carpet tickled the soles of his feet. He stayed in that position, motionless, like a CPU waiting to boot up.

Have to get up some time, he thought.

He stood up and stretched his arms, trying to loosen his stiff muscles and work the circulation back into his body.

Cole shuffled to the window, his balls itching, right hand doing a little scratch-scratch-yank number. He parted the heavy curtains, and sunlight shot in the room, blinding him for a brief second.

Must have been nine or ten o'clock. He surveyed the street below through his third floor apartment window – the Mini Mart and Ace's Barber Shop across the street, the public phone booth with a busted payphone the city had never replaced, and the dumpster in the alley were all visible as usual. His Toyota pickup truck still lay on its side like a giant bug that had keeled over and died.

And the zombies, of course. He took note of them too.

***

Cole showered and toweled off.

He'd been living in this crappy apartment for close to three weeks now – two weeks longer than most people were expected to survive after the zombie shit storm.

2

Cole made up that bit of statistics himself, but it was probably accurate. Sure as hell felt that way. Besides, it wasn't like there was anyone to refute his data gathering methodology.

Zombies. Flesh-eating bags of animated, rotting meat. Christ. He bet no one saw that coming. Multi-million-dollar companies were too busy developing new potato chip flavors, and humanity was too engrossed in the next *American Idol* and the next *Master Chef*.

Shame. If only great vocal cords and perfectly poached eggs could fight off the undead.

Cole put on a clean pair of boxer shorts and jeans. He was lucky the apartment's previous owner was about the same size he was. No taste in clothing though. Cole slipped into a red Hawaiian shirt with palm frond print. He buttoned the shirt and studied himself in the mirror.

Christ.

Food. Clothing. Shelter.

Man's basic needs and Cole had all three.

He caught another glimpse of his reflection in the Hawaiian shirt and shook his head. Okay, maybe two out of three.

***

When the zombie apocalypse hit, Cole thought the most important thing to do was secure a weapon. A pistol, a shotgun, maybe even something old school like a tire iron or a machete.

But he was wrong. Sure, arming yourself was crucial; but guns ran out of bullets, and arms tired eventually.

When all was said and done, you needed shelter from the undead. Preferably one with a thick, hardwood door and a deadbolt.

Equally important was the matter of food. Cole wasn't delusional. He knew his chances of ordering another fillet mignon with a side order of buttered young corn were slimmer than an Olsen twin waistline.

Somehow, he'd managed. Quite well, in fact. When he'd "moved in," one of the apartment's cabinets was stocked with Cheetos, canned tuna, pretzels, a jar of pickles, and a bag of salted macadamia nuts.

But that was weeks ago. Now he was down to two pickles and a can of tuna.

As much as he hated the idea, it was time for a food run.

***

The building was three storeys tall, each floor housing an apartment unit.

Cole had already checked the units below. Both were empty when he'd arrived. The first one was probably owned by a female. He found scented candles and a dozen pictures of a tabby cat. No sign of the woman or the cat though. What he did find was a tube of toothpaste and a bottle of shampoo. He pocketed both. The shampoo smelled of jasmine, but he didn't complain. It beat having lice or ticks. Cole didn't have either, so at least he had that going for him.

The apartment on the second floor was a bit disturbing. It was locked, so after knocking and getting no answer, Cole had kicked the door to gain entry.

Inside the bedroom drawer, he found a pair of handcuffs, a gag ball, a box of condoms, and a half-empty bottle of lubricant.

He couldn't wait to get out of there.

When he was twelve, he had a turtle named Baxter. A red ear about the size of his palm, Cole kept the little guy in a small glass bowl with a couple of green plastic soldiers to keep the reptile company.

He fed the turtle pellets he'd purchased from a nearby pet shop. Twice a week, he changed the water inside the bowl and scrubbed Baxter's shell with a small toothbrush.

One afternoon, Cole came home from school and found the turtle dead.

Death was still an unfamiliar concept to him at the time, and he had cried at the loss of the reptile. Baxter had been more than a pet. He'd been Cole's friend.

"Wake up, Baxter," he sobbed. "Come on, buddy. Wake up."

"He's dead, kiddo," his father said. "He's not waking up. The dead stay dead."

***

Cole surveyed the street through a glass pane embedded on the front door and counted four zombies shambling in front of the building.

Four, he could handle. The undead were generally slow, but who knew how many more were waiting for him inside the convenience store and the barber shop?

His gaze settled on the pickup, and he felt a twinge of sadness. He spent a lot of hours on that truck, working on its engine and installing a kick-ass sound system. It pissed him off seeing it like that.

Cole's right hand tightened around the wooden club that had once been a table leg. It was a crude weapon and made him feel like a caveman, but its weight reassured him. He imagined himself storming outside and screaming, "Come get some!"

Probably not the brightest idea. Zombies weren't quick on their feet, but their feral snarls attracted more of their kind.

Cole backed away from the door. He needed more than just a table leg for this little operation.

He turned and hurried up the stairs, taking two steps at a time to the pervert's apartment. He didn't want to go back in there, but he needed to be well-above street level for what he had in mind.

Cole set the table leg by the door and made a beeline for the perv's kitchen. He opened a cabinet and hit the jackpot on the first try.

Fun Fact: The thing folks hardly brought with them when they evacuated? Glassware. That and silverware. This made sense, because why burden yourself with something heavy? Who were you expecting for dinner?

He grabbed five large plates, careful not to break them. Cradling them in his arms, he headed for the window overlooking the street below. He set the dishes on the floor and slid the glass pane open.

No wind. Good.

The four zombies continued to roam the street that lay between the building and the Mini Mart. They wandered around, following a route that lacked any true direction – a yellow brick road that only their rotting brains could see.

Cole picked up one of the plates and tested its weight. He looked out the window, needing a target.

The fire hydrant at the corner. Perfect.

You can do this, he said to himself. *It'll be just like throwing a Frisbee.*

He twisted his waist, his right hand across his chest, and sent the plate flying out the window.

Heads up!

Like a miniature flying saucer, the plate soared through the air. It landed on the pavement and shattered into a dozen pieces. He'd missed the hydrant by a couple of feet, but he wasn't really expecting to hit it. That was close enough.

The sound of breaking glass traveled through the street.

The reaction was almost instantaneous. The zombies stopped and cocked their heads, looking confused.

Cole picked up another plate and let it fly.

This one was dead on. The plate exploded against the hydrant, and he resisted the impulse to cheer. He allowed himself a smile, though. He was pretty good at this.

The zombies took the bait. They marched down the empty street toward the hydrant to investigate.

This was Cole's chance. He ran out of the apartment, retrieving the table leg by the door, and hurried down the stairway.

Staying low, Cole crossed the street. He ducked behind the pickup and peered around the hood.

The four zombies circled the hydrant, unsure what to make of it.

He sprinted to the Mini Mart. He could hear his heartbeat in his head.

Lub dub, lub dub, lub dub, lub dub…

He pushed through the door, offering a silent prayer of thanks that it was unlocked.

Cole raised the club like a baseball player stepping up to a plate. If any of the undead were in here with him, they'd be getting a crash course in Lumber 101.

He waited for a few seconds, but it felt like several minutes. Nothing attacked him. No monsters in Aisle 5. Satisfied that he wasn't in any immediate danger, he reached in his left pants pocket to pull out a folded plastic bag and started down the first aisle.

He hadn't prepared a shopping list, so he just grabbed whatever he could find – packets of peanut-flavored M&M's, a box of Chips Ahoy!, a bag of marshmallows, Cheez Whiz, a loaf of bread, canned pineapple chunks, and, because they were there, a bottle of mouthwash and a pack of gum. He also stuffed a Butterfinger in his pocket.

He lifted the plastic bag, estimating its weight.

It was time to go.

***

Back at the apartment, Cole chewed a stick of gum by the window, an empty packet of M&Ms on the floor.

The fearsome four had returned to the front of the Mini Mart.

What was it with those things? Didn't they have zombie families to go home to?

A scene played in Cole's mind.

"Where in the world have you been, Hubert? The kids and I have been worried sick."

"Nowhere, dear. The guys and I were just hanging out at the Mini Mart, and I lost track of time."

"What so great about that place? I swear you always act like hanging out with your guy friends is more important than spending time with your family. I can't take this anymore, Hubert. This has to stop."

Cole shook his head and stuck the chewed up gum on the window sill.

That Hubert was such a dick.

***

Evening came as it always did. The entire planet had gone to hell, but the wheels of time kept spinning.

Beauty was only temporary, and cities crumbled. Time did not pause just because you were having a bad day. Even life, with all its complexities, could end in an instant. All it took was an unguarded moment, a drunk driver, an airline pilot off his psychiatric meds, a distraught co-worker at the office, or a bad plate of sushi.

The truth was that time didn't give a shit about anyone or anything.

He was back in the basement in San Vicente. Cole had never known darkness like that. Blackness was all around him, almost fluid, like oil.

8

Cole knew the darkness could not hurt him, but a lifetime of horror movies and reruns of *The Walking Dead* didn't help.

Footsteps overhead. He knew who they belonged to.

Paula, Cole's neighbor. Except she was not Paula anymore. Not the sultry bombshell who majored in Fine Arts. Not the blonde-haired fantasy who took to wandering topless in her home.

That thing pacing back and forth across the living room was a monster hell bent on eating him alive. Or at least until he, too, became one of the undead.

Cole had no intention of giving her the opportunity, no matter how many times he had peeked in her window and gazed at her boobs in the past.

He knew no one would hear him scream down here. Damn if that didn't sound like a line from a cheesy horror film.

Getting to the phone was not an option. He did not own a cell, and he doubted Paula would grant him a five-minute break to phone a friend if he did.

One thing at a time. Get out of the basement first. He'd worry about finding help later.

Cole groped in the darkness so black that he felt like he was breathing it in. He couldn't even see his hands.

Would the grief-stricken Oedipus have agreed with his assessment or laughed at him?

You want to know what true darkness is, my boy? Try gouging your eyes, and then we'll talk.

He bumped into a vertical support beam and winced.

Should have changed that damn light bulb two days ago.

At least he knew where he was now. In his mind's eye, he pictured the basement. Cole reached out with his left arm and felt the cool edge of the worktable. He swept his hand across the top, knocking over a plastic container. Nails and screws clinked on the floor like a pocketful of change.

His hand brushed against a length of smooth wood. Cole gripped the handle of the hammer and steeled himself.

Okay. Get out of the cellar first. Worry about finding help later.

Cole turned a hundred and eighty degrees and advanced four steps until he reached the base of a set of stairs. Using the wooden railing, he ascended the steps, each plank creaking under his weight. Afraid the noise would attract Paula, he stayed close to the rail. He'd read somewhere it would reduce the noise.

It worked. Soon, the man found himself on the top step. He turned his head and pressed his ear against the door.

A shuffling could be heard behind it. One moment, it sounded like Paula was directly outside the basement door. A minute later, the sound receded as Cole's undead neighbor moved towards the other end of the living room.

When the footsteps receded once more, he wrapped his hands around the doorknob and twisted.

***

Cole opened his eyes. He knew morning had not yet arrived because the room was still cold.

He had grown accustomed to sleeping in the dark. The zombies, or whatever those things were outside, were drawn to sound and light.

Cole used to hear the occasional gunshot. Sometimes, a random scream. There were none of those tonight. In fact, he had not heard anything in over a week.

He did not know what terrified him more – the gunshot and screams, or the dead silence.

***

He woke with a start.

A gunshot.

He listened. Perhaps he had imagined it. Or dreamt it. A random sound that had managed to pierce the veil between dreams and wakefulness. He was about to go back to sleep when he heard it again. A pop. Closer this time.

His breath caught. He tumbled out of bed and hurried to the window. Cole swiped the curtains and hissed as the sunlight stung his eyes.

He scanned the streets frantically, not sure what he was looking for but knowing he would recognize it when he saw it.

There! A man sprinted down the street, and he was alone. Cole guesstimated a dozen zombies chasing after him. The stranger turned and raised what looked like a pistol. He fired, and a zombie in a red baseball cap planted its face on the sidewalk.

Without a second thought, Cole picked up his club and dashed out of the apartment. The guy probably didn't have many bullets left. Not that it mattered if he did.

Everyone ran out of bullets eventually.

Cole was not sure what he was going to do once he reached the ground floor. *I'll cross that bridge when I get there,* he said to himself.

He barely had time to stop when he reached the front door. He stuck his face against the glass pane.

"Come on. Where the hell are you?" he mumbled, his breath fogging the glass.

As if on cue, the man appeared across the street. As far as Cole could tell, the stranger was in his mid- or late fifties. He looked exhausted. Another two or three blocks and he'd have a heart attack. The man's undead fan club was gaining on him, though. He probably wouldn't make it that far.

Sometimes, the hardest decisions in life involve choosing whether to do something or walk away.

Cole hoped he wouldn't regret what he was about to do.

11

He opened the door. "Hey!" he yelled. "This way!"

Cole literally pulled the guy off the street, grabbing the man's hand and yanking him inside the building. Once they were both inside, Cole slammed the door and engaged the lock and the security chain.

"Lock it, lock it!" the stranger panted, his eyes wild.

"Relax! It's locked."

"Thank you. Christ Almighty, I thought I was done for."

The guy wore some sort of security uniform. He still held the pistol by his side, and Cole could not take his eyes off the weapon. It made him nervous.

The older man licked his lips, transferred the gun to his left hand, and extended his right. "Thanks again for saving my ass. Name's Marshall."

Cole took the man's hand and shook it. Marshall's grip was firm and strong, and his fingers were calloused. This guy was no slouch.

"Good to meet you. That your first or last name?"

"Last," he answered, still breathing heavily.

"I'm Cole." He did not know what else to say, so he added, "That's my first name."

Marshall did a quick glance over his shoulder. "Where are the rest?"

"Sorry, I'm not following you. The rest of what?"

"The rest of your crew."

Cole frowned. "I'm not sure what you were expecting, but I'm the only one here."

The news seemed to disappoint Marshall. He'd have been more than disappointed if he had ended up an all-you-can-eat meal for the zombies outside.

Something slammed against the door, and Cole spun around. Pressed against the glass pane, like a Jehovah's Witness on a mission, was an old lady in a sun hat. She gnashed her dentures at him.

"Come on," Cole said, brushing past Marshall. "Help me find something to brace the door."

His new companion followed without complaint.

***

"Is that a table leg?" Marshall asked.

After barricading the building's front entrance with a coffee table and two chairs, the pair retreated to Cole's apartment on the third floor.

"Yes."

"A little bit crude, don't you think?"

"Yeah, well, I left my proton cannon at home."

Touchy. Cole had lost his people skills.

Not that he was much different before all this started. He had pretty much kept to himself. Didn't even own a dog.

"Sorry," Marshall said. "I didn't mean anything by it."

"No, no. My fault." Cole took a deep breath and did his best to smile. Couldn't quite pull it off. "I don't get a lot of visitors, that's all."

They stared at the floor, neither of them saying anything.

Cole cleared his throat and gestured at Marshall's uniform. "What exactly do you do?"

"I work for a security agency. Well, used to anyway. Antaeus Security. We provide security detail for government officials and high-profile personalities."

Marshall caught Cole raising an eyebrow. "I know what you're thinking. I haven't been out in the field in over six years. Been stuck behind a desk job doing consultations, mostly. Used to be able to run five miles on a bad day. Now, I can barely outrun a bunch of dead guys." He looked down at his pistol. "I can still shoot pretty well, though."

"How many bullets are in that thing?"

Cole wasn't a gun expert but guessed it might have been a .45 or a 9mm.

"Four. Maybe five. I should've taken the M4, or at least a shotgun, but when the Chevy ran out of fuel, those things got the jump on me. I barely got out—"

13

"Wait a minute," Cole interrupted, his body in attention. "You have a shotgun and an M4?"

Marshall nodded. "Two shotguns, actually; -and a couple more side arms. I was at the office when I saw what was happening on the news. Rodney and Christian cut and ran.

"They took most of the guns, but even they couldn't take everything. Figured I'd help myself."

Cole had no idea who Rodney and Christian were, but the gears in his brain were already turning. "Where exactly did you say your car broke down?"

He couldn't keep still. He was a child's toy wound too tightly – one of those small monkeys holding a pair of tiny cymbals. He paced around the apartment. At any moment, a spring would snap. Damn, he needed a cigarette. He made a mental note of it for his next food run.

***

"Mabini Street?" Cole asked.

Marshall sat on a chair, nibbling on a Chips Ahoy! cookie, a half-empty glass of water in front of him. He nodded. "Three blocks down."

Cole went back to pacing. "And how many zombies would you say there were?"

"I didn't exactly have time for a head count." Marshall leaned forward and drank the rest of his water. "Listen to me, Cole. There's no telling how many of those bastards are out there. A few dozen? Could be a hundred. I barely made it out of there."

"Yeah. That's why I should go alone. No offense, but you'd only slow me down."

Damn his people skills again. His mother would have been so proud.

Fortunately, Marshall didn't look angry. In fact, the guy appeared to consider it. If anything, he was a practical man and placed logic ahead of pride.

Cole stared out the apartment window, in the direction of Mabini. He imagined the Chevy parked along the road, the backseat packed with the small arsenal Marshall described.

"Let me ask you a question," the older man said. He got off the chair and walked towards Cole. "Say you do get to my car. A couple of shotguns, a rifle, some handguns, and ammunition…

"You gonna carry all that with you? Last time I checked, those things aren't exactly lightweight."

"I never said I was carrying anything," Cole answered. He grinned. "I'll drive back."

Marshall sighed. He seemed to have aged five years in the past five minutes. "The Chevy's out of fuel, remember? I wouldn't be here if it wasn't. You plan on pushing my car to the nearest Petron station?"

Cole smiled. He had already considered that. He motioned the older man beside him and pointed out the window. "No. I figured I'd do better than that."

Marshall stared at the Toyota lying on its side across the street. Cole's truck.

"That yours?" Marshall asked.

Cole nodded.

"Jesus, where'd you learn to drive?"

"Not important." Cole turned to him. "Anyway, I figure I can siphon a gallon of fuel from the tank and take it to your car. That's more than enough fuel to get here."

A smile crept on Marshall's face. He extended his arm and squeezed Cole's shoulder. "We could have used someone like you back in the agency."

Cole shook his head. "Nah. I've got too many traffic violations. Heck, look at how I parked my truck. Also did a bunch of stuff I'm not particularly proud of, including streaking across the field during a high school football game once."

"No kidding? High school?"

Cole shrugged. "I was young and stupid. A buddy bet me a six-pack of beer. Said I couldn't do it."

"But you did."

"Yeah. And that jerk still owes me a six-pack."

Marshall laughed. Cole couldn't help it and laughed along with him.

For a brief moment, they put all thoughts of danger and the creatures lurking outside the building behind them.

***

It was one of those dreams void of sound. Like you were watching a movie on TV, and you accidentally sat on the remote and pressed the mute button.

No longer in the basement.

The windshield. The steering wheel. Keys in the ignition. It took him a moment to realize where he was.

He was inside the Toyota. In the driver's seat.

Cole breathed a sigh of relief.

He noticed his hands. What the hell was on them? Like oatmeal and chocolate syrup. The brown liquid snaked down his arm and trickled off his elbow onto the matted floor.

Where was his hammer?

He turned his head, and immediately wished he hadn't. Paula's head stuck inside the truck, her neck lodged, caught in the window. She looked like a half-born baby stuck inside a birth canal.

He found the hammer. The claw was buried deep in Paula's ruined skull. Oatmeal dripped off the wooden handle.

Cole opened his mouth and screamed in silence.

His eyelids fluttered open. Instead of darkness, sunlight filled the bedroom.

"Bad dream?"

"Yeah," Cole groaned. He sat up against the headboard and rubbed the sleep from his eyes.

Marshall stood by the window. "Sounded like it might've been. Who's Paula?"

"Someone I used to know," Cole answered. He didn't want to get into it. A tale of bashing skulls was never a good way to start the day. "You sleep well?"

The older man continued staring out the window. "Couldn't sleep. The apartment on the ground floor was too close to the front door, and the one on the second floor kind of freaks me out."

Cole chuckled. "I know exactly what you mean."

"Since you're already up, you better come take a look at this."

Cole dragged himself out of bed and walked to the window. He froze.

Until a day ago, there had only been four zombies. Now, there were over ten of them. He spotted the old lady in the sun hat from yesterday.

"I can't help but feel this is my fault," said Marshall.

Cole wanted to say something along the lines of "duh!" or "no shit!" but he didn't. The truth was, he liked Marshall. Despite their age difference, the guy was a survivor just like he was.

"Don't beat yourself up over it. Things could be worse."

The old man looked at him. "Oh, yeah? How?"

Cole thought about it. "Well, for starters, you could be the guy who owns the apartment downstairs."

After a quick check of the front door to make sure none of the zombies had broken into the building, they returned to Cole's apartment, pulled up two chairs, and sat by the window.

They passed two packets of M&Ms and a can of pineapple chunks between each other. After they had devoured the fruit, they took turns sipping the sugary syrup left in the can.

"You still wanna go through with it?" Marshall asked.

"Been thinking about it," Cole admitted. "I need a few things first."

"You doing it today?"

"Today. Tomorrow. What difference does it make? Might as well be today."

The old man's expression was grim. "Look, Cole, I'm not going to tell you what to do. You've obviously gotten by pretty well on your own. But how do you plan to get to your truck without those zombies seeing you?"

"Been thinking about that, too, and I'm glad you asked because I'll need a bit of an assist."

Cole recounted the incident involving the zombies and the plates. When he was done, Marshall was staring at him, his mouth open.

"And it actually works?"

"Zombies aren't the smartest creatures. Maybe their brains aren't getting enough oxygen. I don't know. But it works."

Marshall chewed on his lower lip. "The zombies just chase the plates?"

"They don't really chase the plates. It's the noise. Makes them curious and distracts them long enough to get the job done."

The older man leaned back in his chair and rubbed his forehead with his fingers. "You're either very smart or very reckless."

"Guess we'll find out which one. Now, when was the last time you threw a Frisbee?"

***

Cole rummaged through the kitchen cabinets of the first floor apartment. It amazed him how many pots and pans the previous owner had. Like he or she was getting ready for some great big cookout.

There was enough metal in here to rebuild Cybertron but nothing of use to him.

He shut the last cabinet. He turned and leaned against the sink. Across the kitchen, the refrigerator hummed to itself. Cole stepped towards it and opened the door.

He took stock of the items – an empty egg tray, celery sticks that had gone bad, and some lasagna that made him sick just by looking at it.

His gaze settled on a half-empty gallon of milk that had exceeded its expiration date. Holding his breath just in case lasagna carried some yet-undiscovered strain of botulism or SARS, he reached in the fridge, grabbed the container, and shut the door.

Dusk had begun to set.

Marshall walked in Cole's apartment. Though technically he didn't own the place, Cole had gotten used to calling it his.

"I dragged a couch and added it to our little barricade downstairs," Marshall said. "We should have no problem sleeping tonight."

"Thanks," Cole said. He sat beside the small dining table, staring at a meter's length of hose and the now-empty plastic milk container.

Marshall set something on the table. "I also found this."

The nightstick was black. Cole had watched police officers use them in movies, but he'd never actually seen one before.

"Where'd you find it?"

The older man settled on a chair across the table. "In the second-storey apartment. It was in a briefcase stashed under the bed. I found it next to a police uniform. The uniform's a fake. You can purchase them online." He pointed at the weapon. "But this is real. I figured you might consider upgrading your table leg."

Cole laughed and picked up the nightstick. "I think you may be right."

"I also found a couple of adult magazines in the briefcase." Marshall grinned. "My guess is whoever was living in the apartment was into some freaky stuff."

"To each, his own, right?"

Marshall laughed. "I suppose. So, what's for dinner?"

Cole replaced the nightstick on the table. "There are some marshmallows in the cabinet. But go easy, okay? We've got to make it last."

Earlier, he realized that with Marshall here, food consumption doubled. That meant more trips to the Mini Mart. At some point, even the convenience store would run out of food.

Marshall sighed. "I could lose some weight anyway."

***

"Mom, when's dad coming home?"

"I really don't know, honey."

"But where is he?"

"Hubert – I mean, your dad is out with his friends at the Mini Mart. Says there are two guys in a nearby building that look delicious."

"When I grow up, I want to hang out at the Mini Mart too"

"Oh, no you won't! You're going to be a doctor or a lawyer. You hear me? Now hush and eat your brains."

***

"I really can't talk you out of it?" Marshall asked.

"Nope, you really can't," Cole answered.

It was about eight or nine in the morning. They stood on the landing of the second floor.

Marshall knew he could not convince Cole into abandoning his plan. He knew Cole's type, the ones who got ideas in their heads and went after them no-holds-barred. They were the guys you elected student president of your high school. The type you swore into office. They were heroes that saved lives.

They were also the type that got themselves killed.

Marshall looked hard at Cole. The younger man did not even flinch.

"Okay," Marshall said, defeated. "Let's go over the plan one more time."

***

The plan was to distract the zombies to give Cole enough time to collect fuel from the Toyota. When that was done, Cole would return to the building, and they would reassess the situation from there.

If anything went wrong, Cole would haul his ass back into the building. No harm, no foul.

They moved the furniture away from the door slowly so as not attract attention.

"Looks like less of them out there," Marshall said, catching his breath.

Cole peeked through glass on the door. Marshall was right. Five of them today – two on the apartment side of the street and three across. A sixth zombie stood beside the Toyota, looking like a customer interested in purchasing a second-hand car at a used dealership.

"Yep, she's a beauty. I know she's lying on her side right now, but we can fix that real quick. Plus, she runs like a dream. Slips in and out of traffic faster than a greased stripper in a mud wrestling pit."

21

Something familiar about the sixth zombie. Cole realized the same zombie had been there since the day he'd moved in the building.

"Hubert," he whispered.

"Who?"

"Nothing. Just a name I gave that zombie next to the truck. I call him Hubert."

"Jesus, kid. You gave them names?

Cole shrugged. "I was bored."

"Don't you think naming those things might make it harder for you to kill them if the situation calls for it?"

Another shrug. "Not really. That Hubert's kind of an asshole."

He held the container and the hose, which he had cut into two different lengths, in one hand and the nightstick in the other. The keys to the Toyota were in the breast pocket of his shirt – a yellow number with surfboards and ukuleles.

"Once the zombies take the bait, I need you to come back down here to open the door for me. I don't want to fumble with the doorknob if I've got a zombie on my ass."

Marshall wrung his hands together. "Got it. You sound like you've done this before."

"What makes you think I haven't?" Cole asked.

Marshall did not ask him to elaborate. He knew Cole must have been involved in some shady activities before the world went to shit. Marshall hoped it was not anything major like murder or armed robbery. Probably not. Cole did not give off that vibe hardened criminals sometimes did.

Besides, his young companion's past did not matter. Not anymore. Not when death had inadvertently wiped the slate clean for everyone still alive.

Or maybe it did matter. After all, in a world teeming with the monstrous undead, it paid to have a different kind of monster on your side.

Marshall surveyed the street from the second floor window. From his vantage point, he had a clear view of all six zombies.

Six, including the one named Hubert.

Marshall shook his head in disbelief. *Cole actually gave it a name,* he thought.

So what? Why wouldn't he? Boredom, loneliness, and isolation were as valid as any other reason. God knew Marshall had come close to choking on one of his own bullets a few days ago. It was like the human soul or psyche – or whatever you wanted to call it – shut off. Self-preservation just wasn't much of an issue anymore. What was the point of surviving if it meant living in a world where even death seemed like a blessing?

But he could not go through with it. He had gone so far as shoving the barrel of the pistol in his mouth, deep enough to elicit a gag reflex, but he could not pull the trigger.

Maybe he was a coward.

Marshall had been in fights where he'd been outnumbered and outgunned. He had been shot once and stabbed twice in the field.

No, it wasn't cowardice. He did not fear death. He was afraid that if he shot himself, he would not stay dead. That he'd come back as something else.

The plates lay at his feet, stacked neatly on the floor. He spotted the hydrant across the street and gauged the distance.

He stooped and picked up a plate.

No, he wasn't going to off himself. He would continue to live no matter how hard things got, and dodge death with every ounce of strength he could muster. And if Death ever got its clammy hands on him, then, man, was Death in for a fight.

***

Cole closed his eyes, steadying himself. Then he heard the first plate shatter outside.

His eyelids snapped open. As one, the zombies turned in the direction of the fire hydrant. Ten seconds later, another plate crashed on the street. Three of the creatures shuffled in the direction of the noise.

No good. He needed all of them to move away from the truck.

Come on, come on!

Another crash. Two more zombies wandered away to investigate.

Which left just one more. The one closest to the truck.

Cole grit his teeth. Hubert was really starting to piss him off.

Another plate shattered. This time, Hubert turned and snarled. Finally, he shuffled after the others.

Cole waited a good ten seconds before unlocking the door. He opened it a few inches, in time to see all six of the undead heading for the hydrant.

He snuck out the door and closed it quietly behind him. He hoped Marshall remembered to open the door for him later.

Staying low, he closed the distance between him and the truck. His knuckles were white around the nightstick. Cole prayed he would not need to use it.

As soon as he reached the truck, he set the plastic container and the weapon on the ground where the vehicle concealed him from the zombies' lines of sight. If any of them returned, however, the game would be up.

Cole quickly fished the keys from his shirt pocket. Luckily, his truck was an older model featuring a lock on the panel to the fuel tank. Facing the chassis, he reached up, unlocked the panel with the key, and then proceeded to unscrew the tank cap.

He heard another plate shatter.

That's right, Marshall. Keep those rotten bastards busy.

He set the cap gently on the ground. Christ, he used to be a lot quicker.

Just out of practice. Don't lose your cool.

Cole took the longer length of hose and slid it into the fuel tank. He pulled out a damp rag from his pants pocket and wrapped it around the shorter length of tubing. Then he jammed it in the opening, creating what he hoped was an airtight seal.

Move, damn you! his mind shrieked.

He took a deep breath and blew into the shorter tube and waited.

Nothing.

Cole blew into the shorter tube again and was rewarded with a trickle of fuel that splashed on the street. He inhaled once more and blew harder. This time, gasoline sloshed out of the longer tubing. He reached down and inserted the hose in the plastic container and watched it fill. While waiting, he peered out the end of the truck and almost stumbled back.

The zombies were returning!

Why? Had they seen him? Was it the scent of fuel? Cole picked the nightstick off the ground. The container was half full, but he needed it completely filled to be sure he had enough. He looked back at the building's entrance. He could not see Marshall, but the guy had to be there. Cole pointed at the zombies as if saying, "Are you seeing this? Do something, dammit!"

Cole expected the door to burst open. Marshall would appear, gun blazing, and the two of them would retreat to the safety of the building.

Except nothing happened. No sign of Marshall.

Bastard! If he got out of this alive, he'd beat Marshall with the nightstick. Better yet, he'd beat the old fart with the table leg. How was that for crude?

Cole's grip tightened around his weapon. If he was dying today, might as well take a few zombies with him. Definitely Hubert. That one *definitely* had to go.

Whump!

The sound took Cole by surprise.

Whump!

What the hell–?

Cole risked a look around the Toyota again. Something was distracting the zombies. They turned like drunken ballerinas and marched in the opposite direction.

Making the most of the opportunity even though he was not sure what had just happened, Cole picked up the almost full container of fuel, screwed the lid on, and hurried back to the apartment. When he arrived at the door, Marshall opened it, shutting it once more when Cole had crossed the threshold.

"I'm so glad you're okay," Marshall said, panting.

"What the hell just happened?" Cole demanded. It took all his self-control not to bash Marshall on the head. "I almost died out there!"

There was obvious fear in the old man's face, but something else was there, too. Embarrassment.

"Look, I did what you told me to do," said Marshall, "but I... I ran out of plates."

Cole looked down and saw what Marshall was carrying. His brows furrowed, and it took his brain a second to recognize the object.

A rubber dildo.

Marshall followed Cole's gaze and stared at the large phallic device in his hand. His eyes met Cole's.

"Like I said... I ran out of plates."

"Saved by a dildo," Cole muttered, shaking his head, yet unable to hide the smile on his face. "That's something you don't hear every day."

Marshall laughed. "Hey, I won't tell if you won't."

***

They sat on the steps of the stairway, eating Cheez Whiz sandwiches. Cole had taken a shower and changed into another Hawaiian shirt. At least this one was dark blue.

Marshall had taken a shower in the first floor apartment. After holding all those self-pleasure devices, he had practically insisted on it. He traded his uniform for a more comfortable Hang Loose shirt. He looked goofy in that top, but it was either that or the role play police uniform upstairs, so it was no-brainer.

They had cleaned up half the loaf of bread in less than fifteen minutes. After Cole's brush with death, they deserved it. If they needed an excuse to indulge a little, this was the time.

Marshall didn't want to break the atmosphere, but there was a question that begged asking.

"What now?"

"Try to figure out how to travel three blocks to your car without getting noticed by the deadheads," Cole answered.

Marshall stood and wiped his hands on the seat of his pants. "Don't even look at me. No way I'm carrying any more dicks for you."

***

After much thought, they agreed night was the best time to do it. Since it was already getting dark, Cole decided to leave the next evening.

No rush.

"I should go with you," Marshall said again like a broken record.

"We already talked about this," Cole replied, his tone laced with impatience. "If things get hairy, you'll slow me down."

"But I have a gun," the older man pressed.

27

"How many bullets are left in that thing?"

"Just four," Marshall admitted. "But four's still better than nothing."

"Not if I have to drag your ass."

That shut Marshall up.

Cole sighed. Christ, he was getting soft. "Look, man, I appreciate your concern. Really, I do. But I'll be fine. Besides, I need you to keep an eye on this place."

"How do I know you won't just take the car and leave me?"

That stung. "That's crazy," Cole said. "I'm not leaving you. Where else would I go?"

They stared at each other. Finally, Marshall stood up.

"Where are you going?" Cole asked.

The former security agent looked over his shoulder. "To get a pen and a piece of paper so I can sketch where I left the Chevy."

***

Marshall claimed he was a good shot, but the guy couldn't draw worth a damn. Cole could not tell which part of the sketch was up or down.

"It's just a rough sketch," Marshall explained.

"Well, it's definitely something," Cole commented. "Any rougher and I'd swear you had a five-year-old draw this for you."

"What are you talking about?" Marshall asked and pointed at a rectangle on the drawing. "You're holding it wrong. Give me that. There! See that? That's us." He tapped at a letter X with an index finger. "And that's the Chevy. I parked it beside the used bookstore."

Cole rolled his eyes. "Then why didn't you just say so in the first place? I know exactly where that is."

***

Though religion was not really in his nature, Cole entertained the idea that he might already be dead. Maybe he had punched out, and this was Hell.

He quickly dismissed that possibility. Not nearly enough people.

"It's silver," Marshall said, handing him a key on a chain. "Guns are in the backseat. You'll need to pop open the fuel hatch from the inside to fill her up. Once you've done that, you get the hell out of there, you hear me?"

"Yes, mother."

"Be serious."

"I am," Cole said. "I wouldn't be doing this if I wasn't."

"Fair enough. What do you want me to do in the meantime?"

"Oh, I don't know. Feed the cat. Water the plants. And tell the landlord we're not paying the bill until he fixes the kitchen sink."

Marshall glared at him.

Cole sighed. "Just wait for me. Streets are bound to get crowded once I drive up. It'll be like a Macy's parade."

"Which is why the plan doesn't make any sense. Maybe we get the guns – and that's a big *maybe* – but we also lead the zombies straight to us."

"Listen to yourself," Cole said. "You're just a bright ray of sunshine, aren't you? Look, we can't just sit around with our thumbs up our asses. What if we have to move? What happens when we run out of food or water? We need those guns one way or another."

Damn, he needed a cigarette.

"Here, take this," Marshall said and offered his gun. "I have a feeling you'll need it."

Cole took the weapon.

"You know how to use it?" Marshall queried. It was a silly question.

"Yeah. Barrel-end makes bad guys go bye bye."

Cole stuffed the handgun in the small of his back. He picked up the container of gasoline and walked to the door.

"Four bullets," Marshall reminded him. "Make them count."

***

Cole crept slowly along the sidewalk, making as little noise as possible. He did not know how well zombies could see in the dark. It was his hope that their vision wasn't any better than his because with little more than the moon and the occasional streetlamp guiding him, he was having a hell of a time navigating along the street.

He looked back to when he had fled San Vicente about a month ago. Driving to the city from the suburbs was a huge mistake, but how could he have known that at the time? There was supposed to be safety in numbers.

Whatever it was – an infection, some biological weapon, the End of Days – it was spreading faster than anything imaginable.

Cole did his best to conceal himself in the pools of shadows scattered on the sidewalk like inky islands across an asphalt sea. He had tucked the nightstick under his belt. Occasionally, it pressed against his left leg, but it did not hinder his movement.

The fuel sloshed around in the plastic container, forcing him to slow his pace. Not the easiest task when every muscle in his body was screaming to break into a mad run to Marshall's car.

The car. Shit. Would he be able to recognize it? It was dark, and other cars lined both sides of the street like giant petrified scarabs.

Worry about that later, he told himself.

He set the fuel on the ground beside a pair of garbage cans. A cat leapt out of one of the bins and scampered across the street.

Good thing too because just as the feline passed the entrance to an alley, a hand shot out and grabbed the animal by its hind legs. The cat spat and clawed. The hand retracted, taking the squirming kitty with it. There was an angry yowl, and abruptly, the street was silent once more.

Cole crouched behind the garbage bins. His hands were shaking. That could have easily been him.

Keep it together.

He waited a minute. Nothing emerged from the alley.

Taking a deep breath, steeling himself, Cole picked up the gallon of gas and inched forward. He noticed a shape a few meters ahead and recognized it immediately. The hydrant. Beyond it was an intersection.

All right. One block down. Two more to go.

***

A few years ago, he saw something some kid had spray painted on a wall.

Fear is a reflex. Courage is a choice.

That was all fine and good, but whoever painted that line had never seen a zombie before.

No matter what anyone said, fear kept you alive. In extreme cases, fear left you staring dumbly at the headlights of a speeding car coming at you at a hundred kilometers an hour. But in most cases, fear ordered you to get the hell out of the vehicle's way. Fear saved your ass.

Nothing wrong with courage either, except the line that separated courage and stupidity was often blurred.

And right now, Cole was not sure which side he was standing on.

A gust of wind sent a flurry of dead leaves and candy wrappers flying. Some of the debris stuck to the fabric of

31

his clothes like windswept survivors hanging on for dear life.

Cole walked past a deserted coin-operated washer/dryer gig. He thought it was odd how issues like clean clothing were not a priority during the apocalypse. If you knew death was imminent, the least you could do is have the decency to die with clean underwear.

He moved on.

Something crunched under his shoe. The sound brought to mind an image of crushed eggshells. He froze. Crouching, he bent down for a closer look.

He'd stepped on a dried leaf. The sound carried through the night like a sneeze in a public library. His pulse kicked up a notch.

Cole held his breath, hand reaching for the handle of the nightstick, and looked up and down the street.

Nothing stirred.

Exhaling slowly, he surveyed the sidewalk. Three calachuchi trees stood at the border or the curb. Beneath the trees' canopies, scattered directly in his path, were hundreds of palm-sized leaves.

Cole needed another route or else risk exposing himself. He grit his teeth. Could things possibly get any worse?

He waited until a passing cloud blocked the half moon, providing him modest cover, before crossing the street. Ducking beside the concrete steps of a building, he set the fuel on the ground to catch his breath.

This stealth thing was harder than it looked. He was glad Marshall had agreed to stay behind. The guy reminded Cole of his old man – stubborn but tough as nails. Cole lost his father to lung cancer years ago. His old man smoked like a chimney, a nasty habit Cole had picked up when he was in his teens.

He had not lit a cigarette in weeks though. That, at least, was something good that had come from the current state of things, but Cole doubted the Man Upstairs had brought about the end of the world just so he'd give up Marlboros.

Keep moving!

Right. He was wasting time. He stepped out into the sidewalk and almost dropped the container.

A fat, bald zombie in a white apron stood less than five yards away. In the wan light, dried blood stains caked his attire. The creature must have worked in a butcher shop, but Cole was willing to bet most of the Rorschach stains on its clothes weren't from cow's blood.

The zombie loomed before him. It had at least three inches on Cole.

It was one big bastard.

Cole pedaled backward and drew his nightstick. He remembered the gun in his back. No, too loud. He had to do this quietly.

He set the container down again.

The zombie bared its teeth at him. A string of yellow saliva drooled from between a pair of bloated, sausage-like lips.

The smell was awful. Cole could not find the words to describe it.

He raised his weapon and pointed it at the monster as if saying, "Well? Come at me, bro."

The creature charged, and Cole swung, bashing the zombie across the face. A pair of teeth sailed in the air and clattered somewhere in the dark like a pair of rolled dice.

A blow like that would have brought a man closer to God, but the creature just staggered back and remained upright.

Cole went low and thrust the butt of the stick against its knee, inflicting damage on the patella.

What are you doing? The head! Aim for the head!

The zombie dropped to its knees. With a beefy hand, it swiped the air. Cole jumped back to avoid it, then leaned in once more to finish what he'd started.

33

This time, he found the mark. The nightstick slammed against the zombie's forehead, causing the cranium to implode with the sickening sound of fractured bones. The butcher crumpled on the pavement, dead.

Well… deader.

Cole glanced around. The streets remained empty. Chest heaving, he stared at the zombie then at the nightstick.

Marshall was right about the weapon. It was much better than a table leg.

Cole picked up the container and stepped past the unmoving zombie. He placed a wide distance between him and the creature just in case.

Still, he kept the nightstick by his side. Butcher boy back there was bound to have friends.

***

Marshall looked out the window on the second floor. The perv's apartment. The window gave him a better view of the street below and nearby buildings. He would have preferred Cole's apartment on the upper floor, but he wanted to be closer to the front door in case something went down.

In case something went down. Marshall grinned to himself. He was old enough to be someone's grandfather, yet here he was, thinking like some juvenile gangbanger.

His hand reached for his pistol, and he remembered he'd given it to Cole.

That boy needs it more than you do, he told himself.

Marshall had not heard a single gunshot since Cole left the apartment building. He prayed that was a good sign.

***

Staying low next to an abandoned Volkswagen, Cole studied the two zombies across the street up ahead. Two females. Just a couple of undead gals shooting the breeze.

Cole pressed his lips together. One more block, and he would be in Mabini.

He considered making a run for it. He could no doubt outrun those two.

And then what? He did not know the exact location of the car, just that it was parked next to the used bookstore. He still had to pour the fuel into the tank.

So, what now?

Cole did not have all night to decide, so when another cloud rolled over the moon, he crossed the street.

***

Something caught Marshall's attention. He squinted. He thought he saw movement by Cole's pickup.

He could have been wrong. A trick of the light, perhaps? An overactive imagination playing games on a weary mind?

He saw it again. There! Two figures hiding behind the truck.

Zombies? Their movements appeared calculated, with purpose. Marshall strained his eyes.

What in the name of–?

***

Two against one. Not good, but he'd faced worse odds before.

Cole backed against a brick building across the street, maintaining a line of vision on the ladies from Hell.

Cole set the fuel down. He planned to rush them, take them down hard and fast. Amateur hour, but he didn't have any options.

Then he saw a trash can lid. A smile crept on his face as a plan started to form in his head.

He lifted the lid by its handle and held it in front of him.

When Captain America throws his mighty shield…

Time to call on the babes.

Armed like a Viking, a club in one hand and a shield in the other – a trash can lid, but a shield nonetheless – Cole struck the lid with the nightstick. Three strikes. Clang, clang, clang.

He struck the round cover loud enough to get the attention of the two zombies, but hopefully, not so loud as to alert any others.

Clang, clang, clang. Almost like a dinner bell.

Come and get it!

The reaction was as he anticipated. The zombies turned and staggered in his direction like lead filing drawn to a magnet. Something odd about the way the one on the left moved (as if shambling wasn't odd enough).

Cole realized one of the creature's shoes was missing. It must have been a podalic nightmare wearing only one shoe, especially if the other one featured a three-inch heel. The rotting Cinderella did not seem to mind, and shuffled onward like a pro.

The zombie on the right was the quicker of the two. Maybe it was the advantage of having appropriate footwear.

Cole hunkered down, blending into the shadows. If he was wrong about these creatures and if they had better night vision than he did, then he was done for. He might as well have been dancing naked in a shopping mall.

Thankfully, he had presumed correctly. There were no snarls or inhuman cries to alert others of their kind. They approached at a steady pace, drawn more by curiosity than by hunger.

Eight yards.

Cole held his breath.

Six yards.

A drop of sweat traced the angle of his jaw.

Four yards.

Cole leapt out of the shadows and attacked. He closed the distance in a fraction a second and brought the nightstick down, smashing the lead zombie's head. He shoved the creature aside with the garbage lid and swung upward like Rafael Nadal delivering a winning backhand.

Cole was aiming for the face of the second zombie. However, because of her footwear – or lack of it – the club struck her neck instead. Despite that, the blow managed to deliver the desired effect. The creature's spine snapped on impact, and the zombie fell dead.

Humility is an attribute that is severely underrated.

People who lack the characteristic are often assholes. And if you've read the Good Book, God detests assholes and has certain ways of dealing with them.

Cole had handled two zombies single-handedly and was pleased with himself. Very pleased.

Which was probably why, as he stepped over one of the bodies to retrieve the fuel-filled container, he tripped over the zombie's foot and dropped the trash can lid.

The cover bounced off the sidewalk. The lid was a giant coin flipping in the air. Except with this particular coin, heads or tails did not matter. He was screwed either way.

A chorus of snarls tore the night. They seemed to come from all directions.

Cole dashed to retrieve the fuel. He broke into a run just as all hell broke loose.

***

Marshall raced down the stairs, his footsteps like machine gun fire.

His mind raced with a dozen questions demanding answers. Who was out there? Were they friendly or hostile? Where did they come from, and what were they doing here?

He reached the ground floor and paused to catch his breath.

Take it easy, old man, he told himself. *You'll give yourself a stroke.*

He held the table leg in one hand, wishing he still had his pistol. Dammit, what was taking Cole so long?

Couldn't worry about that now.

During the zombie apocalypse, the last thing you expected to hear was a knock on the door.

And that is exactly what Marshall heard.

***

Cole's feet pounded on the pavement. His lungs sucked the cold night air, and his muscles were turning to paste.

Running was hard, but doing it while carrying a gallon of gasoline with fifty zombies on your ass? Now *that* was a bitch.

He wanted to kick himself for being such a klutz, but now was not the time. Besides, if the zombies caught up with him, he would not need to.

Most of the creatures were slow, but others – probably the younger ones or those in earlier stages of decay – were quicker.

Cole wheeled around and swung the nightstick. The weapon struck a zombie – one wearing a three-piece suit – on the shoulder. Not a lethal blow, but the impact sent the zombie slamming into a lamp post with a ding.

Cole did not have the luxury of finishing the creature off. He turned and hightailed it out of there.

***

Marshall stared at the door as if it were something completely alien.

The knocking came again, waking him from his trance. Cautiously, he moved towards the entrance. The sound was so ordinary, so benign, that it was somehow out of place.

Marshall had never known the undead to knock.

"Who is it?" he whispered.

"Oh, thank God!" A woman's voice. "Please help us. My husband… he's hurt."

Marshall's pulse quickened. Survivors!

Could it be? He may not have known if zombies were capable of knocking, but he knew they did not talk.

He reached for the lock but stopped himself.

The woman had said her husband was hurt.

Marshall peeked through the glass and saw the faces of a woman and a man in their thirties. They looked terrified. A bit ragged and dirty, but definitely not zombies.

"Your husband," he inquired, "has he been bitten?"

"No! Nothing like that, I swear," said the woman. "He fell and twisted his ankle. Please let us in. We're begging you."

Marshall did not give it another thought. He unlocked the door and opened it for the couple. He was sure there was a first aid kit somewhere in the building. He hoped the husband's injury was not serious.

The next thing he knew, he was staring down the barrel of a gun.

***

Mabini Street.

He made it!

Cole had managed to put some distance between himself and the hungry mob of the undead, buying himself a few precious seconds.

The used bookstore was up ahead. Cole slowed his pace, worried that he would miss Marshall's car. Wouldn't do if he had to double back.

Sweat dripped down his neck, soaking his shirt. His heart slammed in his ribcage, making it difficult to focus.

Various vehicles flanked Mabini – a Honda City, a station wagon, even a delivery van for Terri's Cakes and Pastries. Cole glanced left and right, searching both sides of the street for the Chevrolet.

He could not find it! Had Marshall lied and sent him on a wild goose chase? That made no sense.

Maybe the old man had been wrong about where he had ditched the car.

A hundred variations of swear words bounced around in Cole's head, but he was too tired, too out of breath to utter a single one.

Suddenly, there it was, nestled under the shadow of a signage for Mr. Quickie's Key Duplication. Cole summoned all his will and made a beeline for the car.

The driver's door was ajar. Apparently, Marshall had left in a hurry, just like he had said. Cole put on a burst of speed.

He skidded to a halt and stuck his head through the open door. He ducked inside the driver's side of the car and pulled the lever that would release the hatch to the fuel tank. Tossing the nightstick on the roof of the Chevy and carrying the fuel, he moved to the rear of the vehicle.

Working quickly, Cole removed the fuel tank cap and set it on the trunk. Then he opened the container of gasoline. The sweet, pungent scent of fuel filled his nostrils.

His hands would not stop shaking. He knew it was due to his body's depletion of adrenaline. It took him two tries to get the mouth of the container inside the fuel tank. The pinkish fluid sloshed and churned as the tank filled itself.

Come on! Get in there!

Cole looked over his shoulder and gasped. The zombies were coming. Initially, he had guessed about fifty or sixty of them. Now he saw he had sorely underestimated their numbers. There must have been at least a hundred out there. He fought off the tidal wave of panic threatening to crush him. He had thirty seconds; a minute, tops.

He had emptied two thirds of the container into the Chevy's tank. It would have to do. Cole prayed it was enough. He replaced the cap of the fuel tank, shut the hatch, and left the plastic container and the remaining gasoline. He had what he came for.

Through the window, he saw the inventory of weapons Marshall had described. Christ! The old man had been on the level. There was enough firepower in the backseat to take over Mordor.

Get in the damn car!

His left hand dug inside his pants pocket for the keys to the vehicle. He retrieved the nightstick from the car's roof and was about to slide in the driver's seat when he detected movement behind him. He spun around in time to catch a male zombie charging from the Chevy's rear. Cole let out a startled cry and brought up the nightstick. The creature tackled him, and Cole banged his head against the inside of the door. Blinking back tears, he fought to stay conscious as pain exploded inside his skull.

He raised the nightstick in the nick of time. The zombie closed its jaws around the weapon like a rabid dog chewing on a bone. Flecks of spittle peppered his face. Cole turned his head and grunted as the weight of the creature threatened to crush him.

He slapped an open palm against the undead male's left ear. It should have been sufficient to rupture an eardrum, but the blow only served to anger the zombie. The creature howled and doubled its efforts, snarling, its breath reeking of decay.

Fuck this! Cole pushed with everything he had and reached behind his back. He drew his gun, jabbed and barrel against the zombie's eye, and squeezed the trigger.

The blast blew apart the back of the monster's head. Gore and blood splattered in all directions. Cole shoved the body off him. He wanted to lie there on the street and close his eyes, but he somehow managed to crawl inside the Chevrolet and shut the door.

***

"Inside! Now!" the man growled at Marshall.

Gone was the desperation they had displayed upon first arriving on the doorstep, replaced by a menacing do-not-fuck-with-us tone.

The husband waved the gun in his face. Was he really her husband? Marshall recognized the weapon – a Beretta 92 or a similar model. This close, a bullet would make quite a mess.

Marshall grit his teeth. Suckered by these two… maybe he *was* too old for the field. He stepped away from the doorway, raising both hands and realized he still had the table leg.

"Drop the stick, Pops," the man ordered.

Pops? Who were these clowns?

The couple entered the building, and the woman closed the door behind them. Marshall heard her engage the deadbolt.

The husband smiled at him. He was handsome, but Marshall imagined a wolf wearing a similar expression if it happened to come across a steak dinner in the middle of the forest.

"It's not a stick. It's actually a –.

Something struck him on the side of the head, and the world went black.

***

Cole locked the doors and not a moment too soon. A zombie dressed in a police officer's uniform collided against his side of the car. The Chevy's frame shook.

No, officer, I haven't been drinking. Promise. No, I swear I have never seen that bag of weed before. Where the devil did that come from?

A second later, another zombie – an Asian woman wearing a barista uniform bearing a nameplate with "Iris" written on it – jumped on the hood of the car. She clawed the windshield, leaving oily stains on the glass.

He had to get out of there before the undead surrounded the vehicle like flies on a big, steaming pile of cow dung.

Cole shoved the key in the ignition and turned it. The engine coughed like a geriatric patient with chronic pulmonary disease. He pumped the gas pedal and turned the key again. Cough, cough, sputter.

"Start!" he yelled, hammering his fist on the steering wheel.

There were three of those things on the hood now. Police Officer Zombie slammed the door again.

Sir, I need you to step out of your vehicle and show me your brain.

Cole tried starting the Chevy again. The engine coughed once more, and with the key still in the Start position, he once more pumped the gas pedal.

Come on! Start, you piece of –

The engine roared to life, and this time, Cole cheered. He switched on the headlights, revealing an entire zombie army blocking the street.

The undead horde failed to dampen his spirits. Left foot on the clutch, Cole shifted to first gear, gripped the steering wheel with both hands, and revved the engine. The Chevy growled at the throng of zombies like a wild silverback gorilla.

Thank God he had always enjoyed *Grand Theft Auto*.

***

Marshall heard footsteps. Sometimes, they were close. Other times, it sounded like they were coming from above.

Strange.

He struggled to cling to consciousness, but darkness pulled him under once more.

***

Cole swerved left and clipped the side of an abandoned Subaru. The impact broke off the side mirror of the parked vehicle and knocked off a zombie hanging on the side of the Chevy.

The car jostled as he mowed through the undead crowd. Twice, the vehicle bounced as the front tires ran over the creatures that were either too slow or too dumb to move out of the way. Cole slammed on the brakes. Two zombies tumbled off the hood. He trampled on the accelerator and ran them over before the pair had a chance to get up.

He knew he was wrecking the car, but he did not think Marshall would mind. After this stunt, he would hotwire any vehicle Marshall picked.

Iris the Zombie Barista still hung onto the windshield. Persistent bitch, that one.

44

He glanced at the rearview mirror. The zombies – those he had not run over – chased after him. They were resilient; he gave them that much. They would never outrun the Chevy, but they would shuffle, crawl, or drag their undead bodies after him if they had to.

The barrier of rotting bodies began to thin, and the car steadily picked up speed.

He shifted gears and raced down the street.

***

Marshall opened his eyes. His return to consciousness brought with it a massive headache. He groaned, rolled onto his back, and found himself on the dusty lobby floor.

He had never been pistol-whipped before.

"Well, looked who's awake," the woman said. She leaned back comfortably on a chair, her legs stretched and propped on a table. "It's the sicko."

Sicko? Was she talking about him?

"What… what are you talking about?" he croaked.

His voice sounded slurred. He searched for the table leg, but it was nowhere to be found. Marshall then tasted blood in his mouth. Must have bit his tongue when he was knocked out. He gingerly touched the side of his head and hissed when his fingers made contact. After examining his hand, he was thankful that it didn't seem to be bleeding.

Anger welled up inside him. He wanted payback.

"You heard Sheryl," the husband said. He sat on the stairs. "We saw your room upstairs." There was a look of disapproval on his face. "You've got issues, man."

He had issues? This coming from the guy who had just pistol-whipped him for no good reason?

Marshall wanted to explain to the douche bag that he did not own the apartment upstairs but decided not to. He did not owe either of these degenerates a damn thing.

"What do you want?" he asked. It hurt when he talked.

"Food," the man answered. "Guns, medicine – anything you've got, we want it."

Marshall massaged his jaw and winced. "I don't have a gun. If I did, I'd have brought it with me when I answered the door."

"You could have hidden it," the man said.

"Why would I do that?"

The guy made a big production of thinking. "Gee, I don't know. Because you're an idiot?"

Sheryl giggled.

Marshal ignored the insult. "As for food, all I have are M&Ms and a couple of marshmallows." He smirked. "There's a Mini Mart across the street, and I've got some money in my wallet. Help yourselves, it's my treat."

"Your money isn't worth shit, Pops," the husband growled. "Look around. Power is the only currency that's worth anything anymore."

Marshall turned to the male intruder but positioned himself so he had a view of both his captors. "Is that why you're out here stealing from other people?"

Sheryl stared at him defiantly. "It's called 'survival of the fittest.' Leo and I are just thinning out the herd."

Marshall laughed. His reaction hurt his head, but he could not help it.

"What's so fucking funny?" Sheryl demanded.

Marshall slowly got to his feet and winced. The room began to sway, but he kept his balance. He was not sure if the headache he had was due to the blow to his skull or these two imbeciles. "You are, that's what. Leo and Sheryl thinning out the heard… Jesus, do you hear yourselves?"

The couple exchanged glances, but Marshall pressed on. "You need to wake up because I'd say the herd is pretty thinned out already. Any thinner and the only people you'll have left are the morons with guns. Not exactly great stock if you're planning to repopulate the world."

The stunned look on Sheryl's face told Marshall he had struck a nerve, but the rage on Leo's face told him he had probably said too much and was going to pay dearly for it.

Leo stood up and strode towards him. Marshall knew what was coming, but he made no effort to run. Leo raised the Beretta and leveled it at Marshall's head.

Outside, there was a high-pitched screech, followed by a deafening crash.

***

Cole jerked back right after Marshall's car ploughed into the pickup. Thank God for safety harnesses.

In the past month, he had crashed two vehicles in the same spot – first the Toyota, now the Chevy.

Had to be some sort of record.

A loud snarl drew Cole back from his thoughts of setting new records for the vehicularly inept.

Son of a bitch!

Beyond the spider web cracks on the windshield, Iris the Zombie Barista remained latched to the Chevy.

Cole's pistol – Marshall's, really – had fallen to the floor after the collision. He undid his seatbelt, reached down, and scooped it up.

Iris pounded on the windshield with her palms. Bits of safety glass rained on the dashboard.

Cole's heart missed a beat. Any minute, the zombie would break in, and here he sat like a sardine in a can.

The apartment building was right across the street. He could open the door and make a run for it, but he'd be lucky if Iris did not get him the moment he stepped out.

He had to deal with that thing.

Where the hell was Marshall? He was supposed to be here. He had to have heard the crash.

Cole stared at the handgun and thought about shooting through the windshield. Three more bullets. Would three shots be enough? Glass made bullets travel funny, and he needed a headshot.

Wait – The guns in the backseat!

He tucked Marshall's gun under the front of his pants.

The barista zombie continued its assault on the windshield. More pieces of glass showered like diamonds in a jewel heist.

He turned around and extended his arm, reaching for the first weapon he could grab. That weapon turned out to be a 12-gauge shotgun.

Cole admired it in the dim light and smiled.

***

Sheryl shot out of her chair and ran to the door.

"What the fuck was that?" she asked.

Leo pointed at Marshall. "You! Don't do anything stupid."

Marshall could have answered that a number of ways but, realizing that all those answers would most probably result in a .40 caliber slug in his head, he chose to remain silent.

"Holy crap!" Sheryl exclaimed, staring out the door. "Leo, you've got to see this. That guy just totaled his Chevy."

The news surprised Marshall. *Cole! The kid made it!*

"Friend of yours?" Leo asked him.

"Yes. Well, not really. I don't know the guy that –"

Leo drove a fist into his stomach. Marshall doubled over and fell on his knees.

"Get up, Pops," Leo said, standing over him. "Let's go greet this friend of yours."

Marshall's legs felt like putty, and they had to help him to the entryway. Sheryl opened the door, and Leo shoved him outside, jabbing the gun against his back, between the shoulder blades.

"No funny stuff," he warned, "or you're dead."

He needn't have told Marshall that. After being pistol-whipped and punched in the gut, he was not in the mood for anything even remotely classified as "funny."

Marshall looked across the street and gasped at the scene before him. Even in the dim light, his Chevy appeared like it had gone through a giant grater.

In fact, the car looked like it had been to Hell and back. Its side mirror dangled like an earring, and the doors were all scratched and dented. It was hard to believe that this had been his car. The fender would also need to be replaced, but the strangest thing about the whole scenario was the female zombie crouched on the hood, pounding like crazy on the windshield. The creature was so engrossed with whatever was inside the car, it had no idea the three of them were there.

Marshall glimpsed movement inside the vehicle. Before he could call out and warn Cole, a blast blew out the front windshield, tearing the zombie apart.

***

His ears were ringing, and the air was thick with the smell of cordite. Maybe discharging the shotgun inside the car was not a great idea.

It got the job done, though. Couldn't argue with results.

The creature lay on the pavement, a tangled mess of limbs and safety glass. Gore pooled beneath its ruined remains.

Cole needed to get back inside the apartment. He tried the door, but it would not budge. Shouldering it did not help either.

Panic coursed through his veins like paralyzing venom. He had to get out fast. Pretty soon, this area of the city would be crawling with the undead.

He checked the locks, realizing he had engaged them when he first got in the car.

Idiot.

Cole unlocked the doors and stumbled into the street. His ears were still ringing. Clinging to the shotgun, he picked himself up and turned to the apartment.

That was when he noticed Marshall. The old man was not alone. Two people were with him – a man and a woman.

Something was not right. Who were they? It was hard to think with all the ringing going on inside his head.

Then he saw the gun.

"Drop the shotgun, mister," Leo ordered.

***

The driver looked at him, then at Marshall.

"I said drop it!" Leo repeated.

"What?" the driver yelled.

"What are you, deaf?" Leo asked.

The driver cocked his head, a confused expression on his face. "What?"

"The shot must have affected his hearing," Marshall said. He cupped his hands around his mouth. "Cole! He wants you to put down the shotgun!"

Cole seemed to get the message. He crouched, carefully set the scattergun on the ground and stepped back. Marshall looked like crap, but after all that he had been through, Cole doubted that he looked any better.

Leo nudged Marshall with the barrel of his gun, and the three of them – Sheryl included – approached Cole and the wrecked Chevrolet.

***

Cole recognized bad situations when he saw them, and this was one of them.

He was not sure who these people were or what they were up to, but he was positive he understood the Cliff Notes version of the situation. If things went sour, Cole knew which direction to shoot.

He kept a close watch on the man and the woman. The guy had a gun, but the female appeared unarmed.

Cole still had the handgun tucked in his waist under his shirt – the same Hawaiian shirt he despised but was now grateful for.

It looked like they had roughed up Marshall.

He backed up slowly as Bonnie and Clyde led Marshall onto the street. Out of the corner of his eye, Cole glimpsed the undead slowly making their way up the road. He had to make a move, but what he needed was a distraction.

Something shifted in the shadows behind Marshall and his captors. Cole noticed it at once, but the three of them were unaware of it, too transfixed on the approaching zombie horde in the horizon.

A figure emerged from the dark, and Cole found himself grinning. He finally had the distraction he needed.

Hubert, you son of a gun! Boy, am I glad to see you.

"Sheryl, sweetie, can you grab the shotgun?" the man called over his shoulder.

Before Sheryl could respond, Hubert clamped his jaws on her shoulder. The zombie shook his head savagely side to side, drawing blood and tearing flesh. The attack was so sudden, so brutal that Cole almost couldn't bear to watch.

Almost.

Sheryl's high-pitched scream caused Leo to spin around. Cole found his opening.

"Marshall! Down!"

For an old guy, Marshall caught on fast. Like a major league baseball player mere yards from the home plate, he dove headfirst to the ground.

Cole reached under his shirt and pulled out the concealed pistol. At the same time, Leo turned and found Marshall face down on the ground. He raised his gun and aimed at Cole.

Cole had one chance to put the guy down. No extra points for marksmanship. Aim for the center of chest and shoot. Nothing fancy.

He held his breath ad squeezed the trigger.

***

Marshall heard the sound of Leo's body landing on the ground. He raised his head and saw blood gushing from a hole in the man's neck.

Leo's Beretta lay a few feet away. Marshall scrambled for it and wrapped his hand around the cool steel. Quickly, he rolled onto his back and shot both Hubert and Sheryl in the head. He had not been kidding. He was one hell of a shot.

Marshall then pushed himself to his feet. The Imperial Army of the damned marched closer.

"We gotta move!" he told Cole.

"Guns are in the backseat," Cole answered.

Marshall passed him and opened the Chevy's rear door. He pocketed the Beretta, leaned in, and grabbed the other shotgun, an M4 assault rifle, a box of shells, and three magazines for the M4.

He hurried back to the apartment and ran past Cole, who stood slack-jawed while staring at the undead horde.

"Snap out of it!" Marshall yelled. "There's more stuff in the car."

"Got it," said Cole, starting for the Chevy.

"Move your ass!"

"I said I got it! I liked you better when you had a gun pointed at you."

Marshall made no comment but smiled. He rounded the three dead bodies and entered the building. Inside, he ran to the table and unloaded the weapons on it.

Had to get the other guns. There was still the matter of a Glock, a Colt .38 Special, another box of shells, and couple more magazines in the backseat. Though he was fairly certain they would be safe inside the building, Marshall preferred being safe *and* well-armed.

He raced out the door and skidded to a stop.

Cole's body was on the ground beside the Chevy, his back leaning against the vehicle's rear tire.

Marshall ran to his friend.

Don't be dead. Don't be dead.

"Cole! What happened?"

His friend's eye fluttered open. "Oh, hey, Marshall. Just taking a breather."

His face was pale. Marshall saw a red stain on Cole's shirt. He had not noticed it before. Marshall hesitated, then touched the stain and held his fingers up where he could examine them.

"You're shot!"

Cole grimaced. "No need to tell me. I already knew that."

"When? How?" Marshall did not know what to say. His speech had been cut down to monosyllabic sentences.

Cole pointed at Leo's dead body, and everything became clear. Before he was shot dead, Leo had managed to get off a final shot.

Marshall wanted to shoot Leo again, kick him until he broke every bone in the guy's body. The bastard deserved it.

Instead, he placed his hand on Cole's shoulder. "We need to get you inside. Can you walk?"

Cole shook his head. "Too late for that. Take the guns and leave me."

"Bullshit! I'll carry you if I have to."

Cole closed his eyes and exhaled as if he were getting ready to take a nap. "Lost too much blood already. This isn't something I can just walk off. Hurry and take the guns."

Marshall tried to think of something he could say to change the kid's mind.

Cole opened his eyes. "See? You're slowing me down already, old man. The guns, Marshall. Now."

The older man nodded and gathered the weapons from the backseat. He gave Cole a final glance. His friend smiled weakly. The pistol Marshall had given him lay in his lap.

"Go," Cole said. "I'll be right behind you."

Marshall smiled sadly and nodded. He sprinted back to the apartment as Cole fired his last two shots into the wave of zombies.

***

Marshall woke up drenched in sweat. He had a nightmare but could not remember what it had been about.

He yawned as he swung his legs over the side of the bed. When he got to his feet, he stifled a groan.

Aging fast, old man, he thought to himself.

He glanced down at the erection that tented the front of his boxers.

Not too old for morning wood, apparently.

Marshall crossed the room, entered the bathroom, and washed his face. He hardly recognized himself in the mirror anymore.

He could not believe it had only been four months since he had ended up in the apartment. Felt much longer than that.

Next, he opened a drawer and selected a white shirt with a cartoon-style painting of a hula girl dancing under a coconut tree.

Breakfast was a peanut butter sandwich and some licorice. He spread some Skippy on the last piece of bread and sighed. He needed to pick up some supplies from across the street again.

Marshall put on a pair of gray sweatpants and laced his shoes. He caught a glimpse of himself and his getup in the mirror as he passed the bathroom.

Maybe he would start a trend.

He picked up the rifle from the dresser, slung it across his shoulder, and left the apartment. As he descended the stairs, he avoided the apartment unit on the second floor. Even after all this time, it still gave him chills.

When he reached the lobby, he strode to the table. On the top was a cloth bag he used to carry items from the Mini Mart. He had even brought back a few magazines. *Good Housekeeping, Reader's Digest, GQ.* It was something to read. Maybe one of these days, boredom would force him to venture to the used bookstore in Mabini.

Not today, though.

He sensed movement beyond the front door.

Taking the bag with him, he walked to the entrance and looked out the dusty glass pane.

Outside, a figure circled the Chevy that had once belonged to him. Occasionally, the figure would turn and glance at the apartment, but there was no recognition in those blank, dead eyes.

"Good morning, Cole," Marshall said, but no one heard him.

END

About the Author

Aurelio Rico Lopez III hails from Iloilo City, Philippines. He is a self-diagnosed scribble junkie whose works of fiction and poetry includes *Far Out*, *Rare*, *A Predisposition for Madness, Kaiju Double Barrel*, and many more.

When he isn't writing, Aurelio enjoys listening to music, drinking coffee, and pretending to purchase doughnuts for his wife when they are really for himself.

Also by Aurelio Rico Lopez III, courtesy of Wild Hunt Press. Get it in eBook or paperback format on Amazon!

www.ingramcontent.com/pod-product-compliance
Lightning Source LLC
Chambersburg PA
CBHW020601130626
46552CB00007B/2990